Clifford and the Moon

by Donna Taylor

Illustrated by Angel Rodriguez

Based on the books by Norman Bridwell

SCHOLASTIC INC.

New York Toronto London Auckland Sydney
Mexico City New Delhi Hong Kong Buenos Aires

Cleo looked up at the moon.

Then she looked in the water.

The moon was there.

"I want this moon," said Cleo.

She jumped into the cool water.

But she could not grab the moon.

"I want that moon," Cleo told T-Bone.

"I will scoop it up for you," said T-Bone.

He dove into the cool water.

But he could not get the moon.

"This moon is hard to get," T-Bone said. "But I will get it soon."

"You should be in bed," said Clifford.

"It is late."

Cleo said, "We know we should sleep. But we want that moon!"

"Hmm, let me think," said Clifford.

He knew his pals would never get the moon.

They would be sad if they did not.

Mrs. Diller called to Cleo.
"Cleo, come home.
It is late."

Sheriff Lewis whistled for
T-Bone to come.

"But we want that moon,"
Cleo said to her pals.

"I will get the moon,"
Clifford said.

Clifford knew just what to do.

He scooped up some water into a pail and he set it down on the sand.

"Come and see what I have for you," he said.

Cleo looked into the pail.

So did T-Bone.

"You did it, Clifford!"
they said.
"You caught the moon
in this pail."

"Yes, I did," said Clifford. "But it's just a trick."

"Then it's a great trick," said Cleo.

T-Bone and Cleo ran to their owners.

It was a good trick, Clifford thought.

What fun to scoop the
moon into a pail of water!